Steck-Vaughn Literature Library
Folk Tales From Around the World

ANIMAL TALES
HUMOROUS TALES
TALL TALES
TALES OF THE WISE AND FOOLISH
TALES OF WONDER
TALES OF TRICKERY
TALES OF THE HEART
TALES OF JUSTICE
TALES OF NATURE
TALES OF CHALLENGE

Program Consultants

Frances Bennie, Ed.D.
Principal
Wescove School
West Covina, California

Barbara Coulter, Ed.D.
Director
Department of Communication Arts
Detroit Public Schools
Detroit, Michigan

Renee Levitt
Educational Consultant
Scarsdale, New York

Louise Matteoni, Ph.D.
Professor of Education
Brooklyn College
City University of New York
New York, New York

CONTENTS

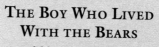

FOLKTALES
FROM AROUND THE WORLD

Tales of the Heart

STECK-VAUGHN
LITERATURE LIBRARY

*This book is dedicated to all folk tale collectors
and storytellers of the past, present, and future,
without whom these stories would be lost.*

Project Editor: Anne Rose Souby
Cover Designer: D. Childress

Product Development and Design: Kirchoff/Wohlberg, Inc.

Editorial Director: Mary Jane Martin
Managing Editor: Nancy Pernick
Project Director: Alice Boynton
Graphic Designer: Richarda Hellner

The credits and acknowledgments that appear on page 80
are hereby made a part of this copyright page.

Library of Congress Cataloging-in-Publication Data
Tales of the heart.
p.   cm.—(Folk tales from around the world)
Summary: An anthology of six folk tales
of love and friendship.
ISBN 0-8114-2408-1 (lib. bdg.)
ISBN 0-8114-4158-X (pbk.)
1. Tales. [1. Folklore.] I. Steck-Vaughn Company.
II. Series: Folk tales from around the world (Austin, Tex.)
PZ8.1.T1468   1990
398.27—dc20   89-11509   CIP   AC

Printed in the United States of America.

4   5   6   7   8   9   0   UN   93   92

CLEVER MANKA

by Parker Fillmore
Czechoslovakia
Page 52

THE GRATEFUL STORK

retold by Yoshiko Uchida
Japan
Page 64

Cap o' Rushes

RETOLD BY JOSEPH JACOBS

Turn the page and enter a world that begins with "There was once" and ends with "And they lived happily ever after." The characters and the plot will probably remind you of other stories you have read.

In this story, you will meet a parent who tests his child's love, a very clever heroine, and a young master who falls in love with a maiden in disguise. All of this awaits you in this tale from merry old England.

WELL, there was once a very rich man, and he had three daughters. He thought he'd see how fond they were of him. So he says to the first, "How much do you love me, my dear?"

"Why," says she, "I love you as I love my life."

"That's good," says he.

So he says to the second, "How much do *you* love me, my dear?"

"Why," says she, "better than anyone in all the world."

"That's good," says he.

So he says to the third, "How much do *you* love me, my dear?"

"Why, I love you as fresh meat loves salt," says she.

Well, he was angry. "You don't love me at all," says he, "and in my house you stay no more." So he drove her out there and then, and shut the door in her face.

Well, she went away on and on till she came to a marsh. There she gathered a lot of rushes and made them into a kind of a cloak with a hood, to cover her from head to foot, and to hide her fine clothes. And then she went on and on till she came to a great house.

"Do you want a maid?" says she.

"No, we don't," says they.

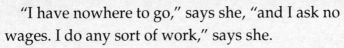

"I have nowhere to go," says she, "and I ask no wages. I do any sort of work," says she.

"Well," says they, "if you like to wash the pots and scrape the saucepans you may stay."

So she stayed there and washed the pots and scraped the saucepans and did all the dirty work. And because she gave no name they called her "Cap o' Rushes."

Well, one day there was to be a great dance a little way off. The servants were allowed to go and look at the grand people. Cap o' Rushes said she was too tired to go, so she stayed at home.

But when everyone had gone, she took off her cap o' rushes, and cleaned herself. And off she went to the dance. No one there was as finely dressed as she.

Well, who should be there but her master's son. And what should he do but fall in love with her the minute he set eyes on her. He wouldn't dance with anyone else.

But before the dance was done, Cap o' Rushes slipped off, and away she went home. And when the other maids came back, she was pretending to be asleep with her cap o' rushes on.

Well, next morning they says to her, "You did miss a sight, Cap o' Rushes!"

"What was that?" says she.

"Why, the most beautiful lady you ever did see! The young master, he never took his eyes off her."

"Well, I should like to have seen her," says Cap o' Rushes.

"Well, there's to be another dance this evening. Perhaps she'll be there."

But, come the evening, Cap o' Rushes said she was too tired to go with them. However, when they were gone, she took off her cap o' rushes and cleaned herself. And away she went to the dance.

The master's son had been hoping to see her. And he danced with no one else, and never took his eyes off her. But, before the dance was over, she slipped off, and home she went. And when the maids came back, she pretended to be asleep with her cap o' rushes on.

The next day they says to her again, "Well, Cap o' Rushes, you should have been there to see the lady. There she was again, and the young master he never took his eyes off her."

"Well, there," says she, "I should like to have seen her."

"Well," says they, "there's a dance again this evening. You must go with us, for she's sure to be there."

Come evening, Cap o' Rushes said she was just too tired to go, and do what they would she stayed at home. But when they were gone she took off her cap o' rushes and cleaned herself. And away she went to the dance.

The master's son was very glad when he saw her. He danced with none but her and never took his eyes off her. When she wouldn't tell him her name, nor where she came from, he gave her a ring. And he told her if he didn't see her again he would die.

Well, before the dance was over, off she slipped, and home she went. And when the maids came home, she was pretending to be asleep with her cap o' rushes on.

Well, next day they says to her, "Cap o' Rushes, you didn't come last night. Now you won't see the lady, for there's no more dances."

"Well, I should like to have seen her," says she.

The master's son he tried every way to find out where the lady was gone. But go where he might, and ask whom he might, he never heard anything about her. And he got worse and worse for the love of her till he had to take to his bed.

"Make some gruel for the young master," they says to the cook. "He's dying for the love of the lady." So the cook she set about making it when Cap o' Rushes came in.

"What are you doing?" says she.

"I'm going to make some gruel for the young master," says the cook, "for he's dying for love of the lady."

"Let me make it," says Cap o' Rushes.

Well, the cook wouldn't at first. But at last she said yes, and Cap o' Rushes made the gruel. And when she had made it, she slipped the ring into it secretly before the cook took it upstairs.

The young man he drank it and then he saw the ring at the bottom.

"Send for the cook," says he.

So up she comes.

"Who made this gruel?" says he.

"I did," says the cook, for she was frightened.

And he looked at her.

"No, you didn't," says he. "Say who did it, and you won't be harmed."

"Well, then, it was Cap o' Rushes," says she.

"Send Cap o' Rushes here," says he.

So Cap o' Rushes came.

"Did you make my gruel?" says he.

"Yes, I did," says she.

"Where did you get this ring?" says he.

"From him that gave it me," says she.

"Who are you, then?" says the young man.

"I'll show you," says she. And she took off her cap o' rushes, and there she was in her beautiful clothes.

Well, the master's son he got well very soon, and they were to be married in a little time. It was to be a very grand wedding, and every one was asked from far and near. And Cap o' Rushes' father was asked. But she never told anybody who she was.

But before the wedding she went to the cook, and says she, "I want you to prepare every dish without any salt."

"That'll taste nasty," says the cook.

"That doesn't matter," says she.

"Very well," says the cook.

Well, the wedding day came, and they were married. And after they were married all the company sat down to the dinner. When they began to eat the meat, it was so tasteless they couldn't eat it. Cap o' Rushes' father tried first one dish and then another, and then he burst out crying.

"What is the matter?" says the master's son to him.

"Oh!" says he, "I had a daughter. And I asked her how much she loved me. And she said 'As much as fresh meat loves salt.' And I turned her from my door, for I thought she didn't love me. And now I see she loved me best of all. And she may be dead for all I know."

"No, Father, here she is!" says Cap o' Rushes. And she goes up to him and puts her arms round him.

And so they were all happy ever after.

Maurice Sendak

ZLATEH THE GOAT

BY ISAAC BASHEVIS SINGER

This story takes place long ago in a small village in Russia. It is December, the time of the Jewish celebration of Hanukkah. Hanukkah is also called the "Festival of Lights." The holiday nearly turns into a tragedy when a boy and his goat are caught in an awful snowstorm. Then, with a little luck and a lot of love, something wonderful happens. And Hanukkah becomes the joyful holiday it is meant to be.

AT Hanukkah time the road from the village to the town is usually covered with snow, but this year the winter had been a mild one. Hanukkah had almost come, yet little snow had fallen. The sun shone most of the time. The peasants complained that because of the dry weather there would be a poor harvest of winter grain. New grass sprouted, and the peasants sent their cattle out to pasture.

For Reuven the furrier it was a bad year, and after long hesitation he decided to sell Zlateh the goat. She was old and gave little milk. Feyvel the town butcher had offered eight gulden for her. Such a sum would buy Hanukkah candles, potatoes and oil for pancakes, gifts for the children, and other holiday necessaries for the house. Reuven told his oldest boy Aaron to take the goat to town.

Aaron understood what taking the goat to Feyvel meant, but he had to obey his father. Leah, his mother, wiped the tears from her eyes when she heard the news. Aaron's younger sisters, Anna and Miriam, cried loudly. Aaron put on his quilted jacket and a cap with earmuffs, bound a rope around Zlateh's neck, and took along two slices of bread with cheese to eat on the road. Aaron was supposed to deliver the goat by evening, spend the night at the butcher's, and return the next day with the money.

While the family said good-bye to the goat, and Aaron placed the rope around her neck, Zlateh stood as patiently and good-naturedly as ever. She licked Reuven's hand. She shook her small white beard. Zlateh trusted human beings. She knew that they always fed her and never did her any harm.

When Aaron brought her out on the road to town, she seemed somewhat astonished. She'd never been led in that direction before. She looked back at him questioningly, as if to say, "Where are you taking me?" But after a while she seemed to come to the conclusion that a goat shouldn't ask questions. Still, the road was different. They passed new fields, pastures, and huts with thatched roofs. Here and there a dog barked and came running after them, but Aaron chased it away with his stick.

The sun was shining when Aaron left the village. Suddenly the weather changed. A large black cloud with a bluish center appeared in the east and spread itself rapidly over the sky. A cold wind blew in with it. The crows flew low, croaking. At first it looked as if it would rain, but instead it began to hail as in summer. It was early in the day, but it became dark as dusk. After a while the hail turned to snow.

In his twelve years Aaron had seen all kinds of weather, but he had never experienced a snow like this one. It was so dense it shut out the light of the day. In a short time their path was completely covered. The wind became as cold as ice. The road to town was narrow and winding. Aaron no longer knew where he was. He could not see through the snow. The cold soon penetrated his quilted jacket.

At first Zlateh didn't seem to mind the change in weather. She too was twelve years old and knew what winter meant. But when her legs sank deeper and deeper into the snow, she began to turn her head and look at Aaron in wonderment. Her mild eyes seemed to ask, "Why are we out in such a storm?" Aaron hoped that a peasant would come along with his cart, but no one passed by.

The snow grew thicker, falling to the ground in large, whirling flakes. Beneath it Aaron's boots touched the softness of a plowed field. He realized that he was no longer on the road. He had gone astray. He could no longer figure out which was east or west, which way was the village, the town. The wind whistled, howled, whirled the snow about in eddies. It looked as if white imps

were playing tag on the fields. A white dust rose above the ground. Zlateh stopped. She could walk no longer. Stubbornly she anchored her cleft hooves in the earth and bleated as if pleading to be taken home. Icicles hung from her white beard, and her horns were glazed with frost.

Aaron did not want to admit the danger, but he knew just the same that if they did not find shelter they would freeze to death. This was no ordinary storm. It was a mighty blizzard. The snowfall had reached his knees. His hands were numb, and he could no longer feel his toes. He choked when he breathed. His nose felt like wood, and he rubbed it with snow. Zlateh's bleating began to sound like crying. Those humans in whom she had so much confidence had dragged her into a trap. Aaron began to pray for himself and also for the innocent animal.

Suddenly he made out the shape of a hill. He wondered what it could be. Who had piled snow into such a huge heap? He moved toward it, dragging Zlateh after him. When he came near it, he realized that it was a large haystack which the snow had blanketed.

Aaron realized immediately that they were saved. With great effort he dug his way through the snow. He was a village boy and knew what to do. When he reached the hay, he hollowed out a nest for himself and the goat. No matter how cold it may be outside, in the hay it is always warm. And hay was food for Zlateh. The moment she smelled it she became contented and began to eat. Outside the snow continued to fall. It quickly covered the passageway Aaron had dug. But a boy and an animal need to breathe, and there was hardly any air in their hideout. Aaron bored a kind of a window through the hay and snow and carefully kept the passage clear.

Zlateh, having eaten her fill, sat down on her hind legs and seemed to have regained her confidence in man. Aaron ate his two slices of bread and cheese, but after the difficult journey he was still hungry. He looked at Zlateh and noticed her udders were full. He lay down next to her, placing himself so that when he milked her he could squirt the milk into his mouth. It was rich and sweet. Zlateh was not accustomed to being milked that way, but she did not resist. On the contrary, she seemed eager to reward Aaron for bringing her to a shelter whose very walls, floor, and ceiling were made of food.

Through the window Aaron could catch a glimpse of the chaos outside. The wind carried before it whole drifts of snow. It was completely

dark, and he did not know whether night had already come or whether it was the darkness of the storm. Thank goodness that in the hay it was not cold. The dried hay, grass, and field flowers exuded the warmth of the summer sun. Zlateh ate frequently; she nibbled from above, below, from the left and right. Her body gave forth an animal warmth, and Aaron cuddled up to her. He had always loved Zlateh, but now she was like a sister. He was alone, cut off from his family, and wanted to talk. He began to talk to Zlateh. "Zlateh, what do you think about what has happened to us?" he asked.

"Maaaa," Zlateh answered.

"If we hadn't found this stack of hay, we would both be frozen stiff by now," Aaron said.

"Maaaa," was the goat's reply.

"If the snow keeps on falling like this, we may have to stay here for days," Aaron explained.

"Maaaa," Zlateh bleated.

"What does 'Maaaa' mean?" Aaron asked. "You'd better speak up clearly."

"Maaaa, Maaaa," Zlateh tried.

"Well, let it be 'Maaaa' then," Aaron said patiently. "You can't speak, but I know you understand. I need you and you need me. Isn't that right?"

"Maaaa."

Aaron became sleepy. He made a pillow out of some hay, leaned his head on it, and dozed off. Zlateh too fell asleep.

When Aaron opened his eyes, he didn't know whether it was morning or night. The snow had blocked up his window. He tried to clear it, but when he had bored through to the length of his arm, he still hadn't reached the outside. Luckily he had his stick with him and was able to break through to the open air. It was still dark outside. The snow continued to fall and the wind wailed, first with one voice and then with many. Sometimes it had the sound of laughter. Zlateh too awoke, and when Aaron greeted her, she answered, "Maaaa." Yes, Zlateh's language consisted of only one word, but it meant many things. Now she was saying, "We must accept all that has been given us—heat, cold, hunger, satisfaction, light, and darkness."

Aaron had awakened hungry. He had eaten up his food, but Zlateh had plenty of milk.

For three days Aaron and Zlateh stayed in the haystack. Aaron had always loved Zlateh, but in these three days he loved her more and more. She fed him with her milk and helped him keep warm. She comforted him with her patience. He told her many stories, and she always cocked her ears and listened. When he patted her, she licked his hand and his face. Then she said, "Maaaa," and he knew it meant, I love you too.

The snow fell for three days, though after the first day it was not as thick and the wind quieted down. Sometimes Aaron felt that there could never have been a summer, that the snow had always fallen, ever since he could remember. He, Aaron, never had a father or mother or sisters. He was a snow child, born of the snow, and so was Zlateh. It was so quiet in the hay that his ears rang in the stillness. Aaron and Zlateh slept all night and a good part of the day. As for Aaron's dreams, they were all about warm weather. He dreamed of green fields, trees covered with blossoms, clear brooks, and singing birds. By the third night the snow had stopped, but Aaron did not dare to find his way home in the darkness. The sky became clear and the moon shone, casting silvery nets on the snow. Aaron dug his way out and looked at the world. It was all white, quiet, dreaming dreams of heavenly splendor. The stars were large and close. The moon swam in the sky as in a sea.

On the morning of the fourth day Aaron heard the ringing of sleigh bells. The haystack was not far from the road. The peasant who drove the sleigh pointed out the way to him—not to the town and Feyvel the butcher, but home to the village. Aaron had decided in the haystack that he would never part with Zlateh.

Aaron's family and their neighbors had searched for the boy and the goat but had found no trace of them during the storm. They feared they were lost. Aaron's mother and sisters cried for him; his father remained silent and gloomy. Suddenly one of the neighbors came running to their house with the news that Aaron and Zlateh were coming up the road.

There was great joy in the family. Aaron told them how he had found the stack of hay and how Zlateh had fed him with her milk. Aaron's sisters kissed and hugged Zlateh and gave her a special treat of chopped carrots and potato peels, which Zlateh gobbled up hungrily.

Nobody ever again thought of selling Zlateh, and now that the cold weather had finally set in, the villagers needed the services of Reuven the furrier once more. When Hanukkah came, Aaron's mother was able to fry pancakes every evening, and Zlateh got her portion too. Even though Zlateh had her own pen, she often came to the kitchen, knocking on the door with her horns to indicate that she was ready to visit, and she was always admitted. In the evening Aaron, Miriam, and Anna played dreidel. Zlateh sat near the stove watching the children and the flickering of the Hanukkah candles.

Once in a while Aaron would ask her, "Zlateh, do you remember those three days we spent together?"

And Zlateh would scratch her neck with a horn, shake her white bearded head and come out with the single sound which expressed all her thoughts, and all her love.

Beauty and the Beast

RETOLD FROM JOSEPH JACOBS

Beautiful maidens and ugly creatures were the characters in some of the earliest folk tales ever told. The creature appeared in different forms. In some stories, it was a frog or a toad. In other stories, the creature was an ugly beast.

A beautiful maiden, her father, and an ugly beast are the main characters in this French folk tale. It is a story of love that is as powerful today as it was long ago.

THERE was once a merchant who had three daughters, and he loved them better than himself. Now it happened that he had to go on a long journey to buy some goods, and when he was just starting he said to them, "What shall I bring you back, my dears?" And the eldest daughter asked to have a necklace. The second daughter wished to have a gold chain. But the youngest daughter said, "Bring back yourself, Papa. That is what I want the most."

"Nonsense, child," said her father, "you must say something that I may remember to bring back for you."

"So," she said, "then bring me back a rose, Father."

Well, the merchant went on his journey. He bought a pearl necklace for his eldest daughter, and a gold chain for his second daughter. But he knew it was no use getting a rose for the youngest while he was so far away because it would fade before he got home. So he made up his mind he would get a rose for her the day he got near his house.

When all his business was done, he rode off home and forgot all about the rose till he was near his house. Then he suddenly remembered what he had promised his youngest daughter, and looked about to see if he could find a rose. Near where he had stopped he saw a great garden. Getting off his horse he wandered about in it till he found a lovely rosebush, and he plucked the most beautiful rose he could see on it.

At that moment he heard a crash like thunder, and looking around he saw a huge monster—two tusks in his mouth and fiery eyes surrounded by bristles, and horns coming out of its head and spreading over its back.

"Mortal," said the Beast, "who said you might pick my roses?"

"Please, sir," said the merchant in fear and terror for his life, "I promised my daughter to bring her home a rose and forgot about it till the last moment. Then I saw your beautiful garden and thought you would not miss a single rose, or else I would have asked your permission."

"Thieving is thieving," said the Beast, "whether it be a rose or a diamond. You must pay with your life."

The merchant fell on his knees. He begged for his life for the sake of his three daughters who had only him to support them.

"Well, mortal, well," said the Beast, "I grant your life on one condition: Seven days from now bring this youngest daughter, for whose sake you have broken into my garden, and leave her here in your place. Otherwise swear that you yourself will return."

So the merchant swore, and taking his rose mounted his horse and rode home.

As soon as he got into his house his daughters came rushing round him, clapping their hands and showing their joy in every way. Soon he gave the necklace to his eldest daughter, the chain to his second daughter, and then he gave the rose to his youngest. As he gave it he sighed.

"Oh, thank you, Father," they all cried. But the

youngest said, "Why did you sigh so deeply when you gave me my rose?"

"Later on I will tell you," said the merchant.

So for several days they lived happily together, though the merchant wandered about gloomy and sad. Nothing his daughters could do would cheer him up. At last he took his youngest daughter aside and said to her, "Bella, do you love your father?"

"Of course I do, Father, of course I do."

"Well, now you have a chance of showing it." And then he told her of all that had happened with the Beast when he got the rose for her.

Bella was very sad. She said, "Oh, Father, it was all on account of me that you fell into the power of this Beast. So I will go with you to him. Perhaps he will do me no harm. But even if he does, better harm to me than to my dear father."

So next day the merchant took Bella behind him on his horse, as was the custom in those days, and rode off to the home of the Beast. And when he got there the doors of the house opened, and what do you think they saw there! Nothing. So they went up the steps and went through the hall, and went into the dining room. There they saw a table spread with all manner of beautiful glasses and plates and dishes with plenty to eat. So they waited and they waited, thinking that the owner of the house would appear. At last the merchant said, "Let's sit down and see what will happen."

When they sat down, invisible hands passed them things to eat and to drink. And they ate and drank to their heart's content. When they arose from the table it arose too, and it disappeared through the door as if it were being carried by invisible servants.

Suddenly there appeared before them the Beast who said to the merchant, "Is this your youngest daughter?" And the merchant said that it was. Then the Beast said, "Is she willing to stay here with me?" And he looked at Bella who said, in a trembling voice, "Yes, sir."

"Well, no harm shall come to you." With that the Beast led the merchant down to his horse and told him he might come the next week to visit his daughter. Then the Beast returned to Bella and said to her, "This house with all that is in it is yours. If there is anything you should want, clap your hands and say the word. It shall be brought to you." And with that he made a sort of bow and went away.

So Bella lived on in the house with the Beast. She was waited on by invisible servants and had whatever she liked to eat and to drink. But she soon got tired of being alone. And, next day, when the Beast came to her, though he looked so terrible, she had been so well treated that she had lost a great deal of her terror of him. So they spoke together about the garden and about the house and about her father's business and about all manner of things. Soon Bella lost altogether her fear of the Beast.

Shortly afterward her father came to see her and found her quite happy. And he felt much less fear about her fate at the hands of the Beast.

So it went on for many days, Bella seeing and talking to the Beast every day, till she got quite to like him. One day the Beast did not come at his usual time, just after the midday meal, and Bella quite missed him. So she wandered about the garden trying to find him, calling out his name, but received no reply. At last she came to the rosebush from which her father had picked the rose. There, under it, what do you think she saw! There was the Beast lying huddled up without any life or motion. Bella was sorry indeed and remembered all the kindness that the Beast had shown her. She threw herself down and said, "Oh, Beast, Beast, why did you die? I was getting to love you so much."

No sooner had she said this than the hide of the Beast split in two and out came a most handsome young prince. He told her that he had been enchanted by a magician and that he could not recover his natural form unless a maiden declared that she loved him.

Thereupon the prince sent for the merchant and his daughters, and he was married to Bella, and they all lived happy together ever afterwards.

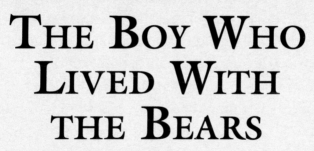

THE BOY WHO LIVED WITH THE BEARS

AS TOLD BY JOSEPH BRUCHAC

Native Americans have a deep respect for nature. Many of their stories of long ago were about animals. Animals played an important part in their lives. They hunted animals for food and used animal skins to make clothing. Some tribes even named their family groups after animals.

This Iroquois folk tale explores a special friendship. It is between a young boy and a group of animals.

THERE was once a boy whose father and mother had died and he was left alone in the world. The only person he had to take care of him was his uncle, but his uncle was not a kind man. The uncle thought that the boy was too much trouble and fed him only scraps from the table and dressed him in tattered clothing and moccasins with soles that were worn away. When the boy slept at night, he had to sleep outside his uncle's lodge far away from the fire. But the boy never complained because his parents had told him always to respect people older than himself.

One day the uncle decided to get rid of the boy. "Come with me," he said. "We are going hunting."

The boy was very happy. His uncle had never taken him hunting before. He followed him into the woods. First his uncle killed a rabbit. The boy picked it up to carry it for the uncle and was ready to turn back to the lodge, but his uncle shook his head. "We will go on. I am not done hunting."

They went further and the uncle killed a fat grouse.

The boy was very happy, for they would have so much to eat that surely his uncle would feed him well that night and he began to turn back, but the uncle shook his head again. "No," he said, "we must go on."

Finally, they came to a place very, very far in the forest where the boy had not been before. There was a great cliff and at its base a cave led into the rock. The opening to the cave was large enough only for a small person to go into. "There are animals hiding in there," the uncle said. "You must crawl in and chase them out so that I can shoot them with my arrows."

The cave was very dark and it looked cold inside, but the boy remembered what his parents had taught him. He crawled into the cave. There were leaves and stones, but there were no animals. He reached the very end of the cave and turned back, ashamed that he had not fulfilled his uncle's expectations. And do you know what he saw? He saw his uncle rolling a great stone in front of the mouth of the cave. And then everything was dark.

The boy tried to move the stone, but it was no use. He was trapped! At first he was afraid, but then he remembered what his parents had told him. If you do good and have faith, good things will come to you. This made the boy happy and he began to sing a song. The song was about himself, a boy who had no parents and needed friends. As he sang, his song grew louder, until he forgot he was trapped in a cave. But then he heard a scratching noise outside and stopped singing, thinking his uncle had come back to let him out of the cave.

However, as soon as he heard the first of many voices outside his cave, he knew that he was wrong. That high squeaking voice was not the voice of his uncle. "We should help this boy," said the high squeaking voice.

"Yes," said a very deep voice which sounded warm and loving. "He is all alone and needs help. There is no doubt that we should help him."

"One of us," said another voice, "will have to adopt him."

And then many other voices, voices of all kinds which seemed to speak in many languages agreed. The strange thing was that the boy could understand all these voices, strange as they were. Then the stone began to move and light streamed into the cave, blinding the boy who had been in the darkness for a long time. He crawled out, very stiff and cold, and looked around him. He was surrounded by many animals!

"Now that we have rescued you," said a small voice from near his feet, "you must choose which of us will be your parents now." He looked down and saw that the one who was speaking was a mole.

"Yes," said a great moose standing in the trees. "You must choose one of us."

"Thank you," said the boy. "You are all so kind. But how can I choose which one of you will be my parents?"

"I know," said the mole. "Let us all tell him what we are like and what kind of lives we lead and he can decide." There was general agreement on that, and so the animals began to come up to the boy one by one.

"I'll begin," said the mole. "I live under the earth and dig my tunnels through the Earth Mother. It is very dark and cozy in my tunnels and we have plenty of worms and grubs to eat."

"That sounds very good," said the boy, "but I am afraid that I am too big to go into your tunnels, friend Mole."

"Come and live with me," said the beaver. "I live in a fine lodge in the midst of a pond. We beavers eat the best bark from the sweetest trees and we dive under the water and sleep in our lodge in the winter time."

"Your life is very interesting too," said the boy, "but I cannot eat bark, and I know that I would freeze in the cold waters of your pond."

"How about me?" said the wolf. "I run through the woods and fields and I catch all the small animals I want to eat. I live in a warm den and you would do well to come with me."

"You too are very kind," said the boy, "but all of the animals have been so kind to me I would not feel right eating them."

"You could be my child," said the deer. "Run with us through the forest and eat the twigs of the trees and the grass of the fields."

"No, friend Deer," the boy said, "you are beautiful and good, but you are so fast that I would be left far behind you."

Then an old she-bear walked over to the boy. She looked at him a long time before she talked and when she spoke her voice was like a growling song. "You can come with us and be a bear," she said. "We bears move slowly and speak with harsh voices, but our hearts are warm. We eat the berries and the roots which grow in the forest and our fur would keep you warm in the long season of cold."

"Yes," said the boy, "I would like to be a bear. I will come with you and you will be my family." So the boy who had no family went to live with the bears. The mother bear had two other children and they became brothers to the boy. They would roll and play together and soon the boy was almost as strong as a bear.

"Be careful, though," the old she-bear cautioned him. "Your brothers' claws are sharp and wherever they scratch you, you will grow hair just like them." They lived together a long time in the forest and the old she-bear taught the boy many things.

One day they were all in the forest seeking berries when the she-bear motioned them to silence. "Listen," she said. "There is a hunter." They listened and, sure enough, they heard the sounds of a man walking. The old she-bear smiled. "We have nothing to fear from him," she said. "He is the heavy-stepper and the twigs and the leaves of the forest speak of him wherever he goes."

Another time as they walked along, the old she-bear again motioned them to silence. "Listen," she said. "Another hunter." They listened and soon they heard the sound of singing. The old she-bear smiled. "That one too is not dangerous. He is the flapping-mouth, the one who talks as he hunts and does not remember that everything in the forest has ears. We bears can hear singing even if it is only thought, and not spoken."

So they lived on happily until one day when the

old she-bear motioned them to silence, a frightened look in her eyes. "Listen," she said, "the one who hunts on two-legs and four-legs. This one is very dangerous to us, and we must hope he does not find us, for the four-legs who hunts with him can follow our tracks wherever we go and the man himself does not give up until he has caught whatever it is that he is hunting for."

Just then they heard the sound of a dog barking. "Run for your lives," cried the old she-bear. "The four-legs has caught our scent."

And so they ran, the boy and the three bears. They ran across streams and up hills, but still the sound of the dog followed them. They ran through swamps and thickets, but the hunters were still close behind. They crossed ravines and forced their way through patches of thorns, but could not escape the sounds of pursuit. Finally, their hearts ready to burst from exhaustion, the old she-bear and the boy and the two bear-brothers came to a great hollow log. "It is our last hope," said the old she-bear. "Go inside."

They crawled into the log and waited, panting and afraid. For a long time, there was no sound and then the noise of the dog sniffing at the end of their log came to their ears. The old she-bear growled and the dog did not dare to come in after them. Then, once again, things were quiet and the boy began to hope that his family would be safe, but his hopes were quickly shattered when he smelled smoke. The resourceful hunter had piled branches at the end of the log and was going to smoke them out!

"Wait," cried the boy in a loud voice. "Do not harm my friends."

"Who is speaking?" shouted a familiar voice from outside the log. "Is there a human being inside there?" There came the sound of branches being kicked away from the mouth of the log and then the smoke stopped. The boy crawled out and looked into the face of the hunter—it was his uncle!

"My nephew!" cried the uncle with tears in his eyes. "Is it truly you? I came back to the cave where I left you, realizing that I had been a cruel and foolish man . . . but you were gone and there were only the tracks of many animals. I thought they had killed you."

And it was true. Before the uncle had reached home, he had realized that he had been a wicked person. He had turned back, resolved to treat the son of his own sister well from then on. His grief had truly been great when he had found him gone.

"It is me," said the boy. "I have been cared for by the bears. They are like my family now, Uncle. Please do not harm them."

The uncle tied his hunting dog to a tree as he nodded his agreement. "Bring out your friends. I will always be the friend of bears from now on if what you say is true."

Uncertain and still somewhat afraid, the old she-bear and her two sons came out of the log. They talked to the boy with words which sounded to the uncle like nothing more than animals growling and told him that he must now be a human being again. "We will always be your friends," said the old she-bear and she shuffled into the forest after her two sons. "And you will remember what it is to know the warmth of an animal's heart."

And so the boy returned to live a long and happy life with his uncle, a friend to the bears and all the animals for as long as he lived.

CLEVER MANKA

BY PARKER FILLMORE

This tale comes from Czechoslovakia. But many stories very much like it are known throughout Europe. In each of the tales, the heroine uses her wits to escape poverty.

In this story, the main characters are Manka and the burgomaster—the town mayor. Manka's wise answers to riddles first attract the attention of the wealthy burgomaster. In time he learns to value her for her fairness and humor, too.

T HERE was once a rich farmer who was as greedy as he was rich. He always drove a hard bargain and always got the better of his poor neighbors. One of these neighbors was a humble shepherd who, in return for service, was to receive from the farmer a cow. When the time of payment came, the farmer refused to give the shepherd the cow, and the shepherd was forced to lay the matter before the burgomaster.

The burgomaster, who was a young man and as yet not very experienced, listened to both sides. When he had deliberated, he said, "Instead of deciding this case, I will put a riddle to you both. The man who makes the best answer shall have the cow. Are you agreed?"

The farmer and the shepherd accepted this proposal and the burgomaster said, "Well, then, here is my riddle: What is the swiftest thing in the world?

What is the sweetest thing? What is the richest? Think out your answers and bring them to me at this same hour tomorrow."

The farmer went home in a temper.

"What kind of burgomaster is this fellow?" he growled. "If he had let me keep the cow, I'd have sent him a bushel of pears. But now I'm in a fair way of losing the cow, for I can't think of any answer to his foolish riddle."

"What is the matter, husband?" his wife asked.

"It's that new burgomaster. The old one would have given me the cow without any argument. But this young man thinks to decide the case by asking us riddles."

When he told his wife what the riddle was, she cheered him greatly by telling him that she knew the answers at once.

"Why, husband," said she, "our gray mare must be the swiftest thing in the world. You know yourself nothing ever passes us on the road. As for the sweetest, did you ever taste honey any sweeter than ours? And I'm sure there's nothing richer than our chest of golden ducats that we've been laying by these forty years."

The farmer was delighted.

"You're right, wife, you're right! That cow remains ours!"

The shepherd, when he got home, was downcast and sad. He had a daughter, a clever girl named Manka, who met him at the door of his cottage and asked, "What is it, father? What did the burgomaster say?"

The shepherd sighed.

"I'm afraid I've lost the cow. The burgomaster set us a riddle, and I know I shall never guess it."

"Perhaps I can help you," Manka said. "What is it?"

The shepherd gave her the riddle, and the next day, as he was setting out for the burgomaster's, Manka told him what answers to make.

When he reached the burgomaster's house, the farmer was already there rubbing his hands and beaming.

The burgomaster again posed the riddle and then asked the farmer his answers.

The farmer cleared his throat and began, "The swiftest thing in the world? Why, my dear sir, that's my gray mare, of course, for no other horse ever passes us on the road. The sweetest? Honey from my beehives, to be sure. The richest? What can be richer than my chest of golden ducats!"

And the farmer squared his shoulders and smiled triumphantly.

"Hmm," said the young burgomaster dryly.

Then he asked, "What answers does the shepherd make?"

The shepherd bowed politely and said, "The swiftest thing in the world is thought, for thought can run any distance in the twinkling of an eye. The sweetest thing of all is sleep, for when a man is tired and sad, what can be sweeter? The richest thing is the earth, for out of the earth come all the riches of the world."

"Good!" the burgomaster cried. "Good! The cow goes to the shepherd!"

Later the burgomaster said to the shepherd, "Tell me now, who gave you those answers? I'm sure they never came out of your own head."

At first the shepherd tried not to tell. But when the burgomaster pressed him, he confessed that they came from his daughter, Manka. The burgomaster, who thought he would like to make another test of Manka's cleverness, sent for ten eggs. He gave them to the shepherd and said, "Take these eggs to Manka. Tell her to have them hatched out by tomorrow and to bring me the chicks."

The shepherd reached home and gave Manka the burgomaster's message. Manka laughed and said, "Take a handful of millet and go right back to the burgomaster. Say to him, 'My daughter sends you this millet. She says that if you plant it, grow it, and have it harvested by tomorrow, she'll bring you the ten chicks and you can feed them the ripe grain.'"

When the burgomaster heard this, he laughed heartily.

"That's a clever girl of yours," he told the shepherd. "If she's as comely as she is clever, I think I'd like to marry her. Tell her to come to see me. But she must come neither by day nor by night, neither riding nor walking, neither dressed nor undressed."

Manka received this message. She waited until the next dawn when night was gone and day not yet arrived. Then she wrapped herself in a fish net and, throwing one leg over a goat's back and keeping one foot on the ground, she went to the burgomaster's house.

Now I ask you: did she go dressed? No, she wasn't dressed. A fish net isn't clothing. Did she go undressed? Of course not, for wasn't she covered with a fish net? Did she walk to the burgomaster's? No, she didn't walk, for she went with one leg thrown over a goat. Then did she ride? Of course she didn't ride, for wasn't she walking on one foot?

When she reached the burgomaster's house,

she called out, "Here I am, Mr. Burgomaster, and I've come neither by day nor by night, neither riding nor walking, neither dressed nor undressed."

The young burgomaster was so delighted with Manka's cleverness and so pleased with her comely looks that he proposed to her at once. In a short time he married her.

"But understand, my dear Manka," he said, "you are not to use that cleverness of yours at my

expense. I won't have you interfering in any of my cases. In fact, if ever you give advice to anyone who comes to me for judgment, I'll turn you out of my house at once and send you home to your father."

All went well for a time. Manka busied herself in her housekeeping and was careful not to interfere in any of the burgomaster's cases.

Then one day two farmers came to the burgomaster to have a dispute settled. One of the farmers owned a mare that had foaled in the marketplace. The colt had run under the wagon of the other farmer. Thereupon the owner of the wagon claimed the colt as his property.

The burgomaster, who was thinking of something else while the case was being presented, said carelessly, "The man who found the colt under his wagon is, of course, the owner of the colt."

As the owner of the mare was leaving the burgomaster's house, he met Manka and stopped to tell her about the case. Manka was ashamed of her husband for making so foolish a decision. She said to the farmer, "Come back this afternoon with a fishing net and stretch it across the dusty road. When the burgomaster sees you, he will come out and ask you what you are doing. Say to him that you're catching fish. When he asks you how you can expect to catch fish in a dusty road, tell him it's just as easy for you to catch fish in a dusty road as it is for a wagon to foal. Then he'll see the injustice of his decision and have the colt returned to you. But remember one thing: you mustn't let him find out that I told you to do this."

That afternoon, when the burgomaster chanced to look out the window, he saw a man stretching a fish net across the dusty road. He went out to him and asked, "What are you doing?"

"Fishing."

"Fishing in a dusty road? Are you daft?"

"Well," the man said, "it's just as easy for me to catch fish in a dusty road as it is for a wagon to foal."

Then the burgomaster recognized the man as the owner of the mare. He had to confess that what he said was true.

"Of course the colt belongs to your mare and must be returned to you. But tell me," he said, "who put you up to this? You didn't think of it yourself."

The farmer tried not to tell. But the burgomaster questioned him until he found out that Manka was at the bottom of it. This made him angry. He went into the house and called his wife.

"Manka," he said, "did you forget what I told you would happen if you went interfering in any of my cases? Home you go this very day. I don't care to hear any excuses. The matter is settled. You may take with you the one thing you like best in my house, for I won't have people saying that I treated you shabbily."

Manka made no outcry.

"Very well, my dear husband, I shall do as you say. I shall go home to my father's cottage and take with me the one thing I like best in your house. But don't make me go until after supper. We have been very happy together and I should like to eat one last meal with you. Let us have no more words but be kind to each other as we've always been. Then we will part as friends."

The burgomaster agreed to this. Manka prepared a fine supper of all the dishes of which her husband was particularly fond. The supper was so good that he ate and ate and ate. At last he grew drowsy and fell sound asleep in his chair. Then without awakening him, Manka had him carried out to the wagon that was waiting to take her home to her father.

The next morning, when the burgomaster opened his eyes, he found himself lying in the shepherd's cottage.

"What does this mean?" he roared out.

"Nothing, dear husband, nothing!" Manka said. "You know you told me I might take with me the one thing I liked best in your house. So of course I took you! That's all."

For a moment the burgomaster rubbed his eyes in amazement. Then he laughed loud and heartily to think how Manka had outwitted him.

"Manka," he said, "you're too clever for me. Come on, my dear, let's go home."

So, they climbed back into the wagon and drove home.

The burgomaster never again scolded his wife, but thereafter whenever a very difficult case came up, he always said, "I think we had better consult my wife. You know she's a very clever woman."

THE GRATEFUL STORK

RETOLD BY YOSHIKO UCHIDA

The Japanese show their love for children and their respect for old people in their stories. Many of their folk tales are about older couples who have no children. Often the main characters are poor fishermen or farmers. In these stories, kindness to animals is rewarded and the couple's wish to have a child comes true.

All of these features are in this tale about an old couple and a stork.

ONCE long ago, there lived a kind old man and woman who were very, very poor. Each day the old man went out to cut wood in the forest nearby, and then took bundles of kindling into town to sell. The old man went out even when snow fell or great icicles dangled from the roof, for if he didn't sell any wood, there would be no money for their food.

One cold, snowy day, the old man set out for the village as usual, with a bundle of kindling strapped to his back. Great soft snowflakes were swirling down from the gray sky, making shapeless white heaps everywhere.

"Ah, how nice it would be to be back home," the old man thought with a sigh. But he knew he could not turn back, and he trudged on down the snow-covered road, beating his hands to keep them warm.

Suddenly, he saw something strange in the middle of a field. Great white wings seemed to be fluttering and churning up a flurry of snow.

"What is this?" the old man thought, rubbing his eyes. "It looks like a snowstorm in the middle of the field."

The old man moved closer, and saw that it was a beautiful white stork that had been caught in a trap. The bird fluttered wildly as it tried to get away, but the more it struggled, the tighter the rope around its leg became.

"Poor frightened bird," said the old man, and even though he was shivering from the cold and anxious to get to town, he stopped to help the stork.

"Here, here," he called gently. "Wait a minute. You're getting all tangled in the rope." And bending down, he loosened the rope around the stork's leg. "Let me untie you quickly, before someone comes along and wants to take you home."

When the rope was undone, the stork beat its great white wings and flew off into the sky. The old man heard it crying into the wind as it soared higher and higher. Then, it circled over the old man's head three times, and flew off toward the mountains.

"Good-bye, stork! Good luck!" the old man called, and he watched until it became a small black speck in the sky. Then, picking up his kindling, he hurried toward the village. It was bitterly cold, but inside the old man felt a warm happy glow. Somehow, the stork seemed to be a good omen, and he felt glad to have helped it get away.

He sold all his kindling in the village and then hurried home to tell the old woman how he had saved a stork that had been caught in a trap.

"You did a good thing, my husband," the old woman said, and the two old people thought of the stork flying home into the hills.

Outside, the snow still fell, piling up all along the sides of the house. "How good it is to be inside on a night like this," the old man said, as he heard the rice sputtering in the kitchen and smelled the good bean soup that bubbled in a pot beside it.

Just then, there was a soft rap-rap-rap at the door.

"Now who could be out on a cold night like this?" the old man thought. But before he could get to the door, he heard a gentle voice calling, *"Gomen kudasai . . .* Is anybody home?"

The old woman hurried to the door. "Who is it?" she called, as she slid open the wooden door. There she saw a white figure covered with snow.

"Come in, come in," the old woman urged. "You must be terribly cold."

"Thank you, yes. It is bitterly cold outside," the stranger said, and she came in shaking the snow

from her shoulders. Then the old man and woman saw that she was a beautiful young girl of about seventeen. Her cheeks and her hands were red from the cold.

"Dear child, where are you going on such a terrible night?" they asked.

"I was going to visit some friends in the next village," the young girl explained. "But it is growing dark and I can no longer follow the road. Will you be good enough to let me sleep here just for tonight?"

"I wish we could help you," the old woman said sadly. "But, alas, we are very poor, and we have no quilts to offer you."

"Oh, but I am young," the girl answered. "I don't need any quilts."

"And we can offer you no more than a bowl of rice and soup for supper," the old man added.

But the young girl just shook her head and laughed. "I shall be happy to eat anything you are going to have," she said. "Please do not worry."

So the old man and woman welcomed the young girl into their home, saying, "Come in, come in. Get warm beside the *hibachi*."

But the young girl went instead to the kitchen where the old woman was preparing supper. "Let me help you," she said, and she worked carefully and quickly. When they had eaten, she got up and washed the dishes before the old woman could tell her to stop.

"You are indeed a good and kind child," the old man and woman said happily, and because they had no children, they wished they could keep her as their own child.

The next morning, the young girl awoke early, and when the old man and woman got up, they found the house swept and the rice bubbling over the charcoals. It was the first time the old woman had had breakfast made for her. "My, you are such a help to me!" she said over and over again.

After breakfast, they looked outside, but snow was still swirling down and had piled up so high around the house, they couldn't even open the door.

"Will you let me stay another day?" the young girl asked.

The old man and woman nodded quickly. "Why, of course," they said. "Stay as long as you like. Since you have come, our house seems to be filled with the sunshine of spring."

Each morning, the three of them looked outside, but the roads were still filled with snow, and the young girl could not venture out. Before long, five days had gone by, and still she could not leave. Finally, on the morning of the sixth day, she came before the old man and woman and said, "I have something I would like to ask you."

"Anything, anything," they answered. "We will do anything you ask us to do, for we have come to love you as our own daughter."

Then, bending her head low, the young girl began to speak. "You see, my mother and father have just died. I was on my way to the next village to live with some relatives whom I do not even know. I would so much rather stay here with you. If you will let me be your daughter, I will work hard and be a good and faithful child."

When the old man and woman heard this, they could scarcely believe their good fortune, for they had prayed all these years for a child to comfort them in their old age. The good gods had surely heard their prayer to send them such a sweet and gentle child.

"You have made us happier than we can say," they answered to the young girl. "From this day on, we will love you and care for you as if you were our very own."

And so it was decided that the young girl would stay with them always.

One day, the young girl set up a small wooden loom in the corner of the room, and put a screen around it so no one could look in.

"I would like to weave something," she said to the old man. "Will you buy me some thread the next time you go to the village?"

So the old man bought all sorts of beautiful colored thread and gave it to the young girl.

"Now," she said. "I'm going to weave something behind the screen. No matter what happens, you must not look in while I am weaving."

The old man and woman nodded their heads. "All right, child," they said. "No matter what happens, we will not look behind the screen while you are weaving."

Soon, they could hear the sound of the girl working at the loom. "Click-clack . . . click-clack . . . swish . . . clickety-clack . . ." The young girl worked from morning till night, hardly taking time to eat her meals, and all day the sound of the loom filled the little house. For three days she worked behind the screen, and finally, on the night of the third day, she brought out a beautiful piece of cloth.

"Look, Ojii-san and Obaa-san," she said, holding up the cloth, "this is what I have been weaving behind the screen."

The old man and woman took the cloth beneath the lamp so they could see it more clearly. It was a beautiful piece of brocade with silver and white birds flying everywhere, their wings flecked with sunlight. The two old people stroked the cloth with their hands and gasped at the loveliness of it.

"It is beautiful!" they said over and over again.

"Will you take it to the village tomorrow and sell it for me?" the young girl asked the old man.

"Why, of course," the old man answered, "although it seems almost too beautiful to sell to anyone."

"Never mind," the young girl said. "I want you to buy me more thread with the money you get for it, and I will soon weave you another one even more beautiful."

And so, early the next morning, the old man carried the piece of brocade to the village. "Brocade for sale!" he called, as he walked down the street. "I have a beautiful piece of brocade for sale!"

Just then, the wealthy lord who lived at the top of the hill was riding through the streets. He stopped the chair in which he was riding and leaned out the window.

"Say there, old man," he called. "Let's see the brocade you have for sale."

The old man unfolded the piece of cloth and held it up for the lord to see. The great lord stroked his chin and looked at it carefully.

"Hmmmm," he said. "This is the finest piece of brocade I have seen in a long time. It glistens like a thousand snowflakes in the sun." Then he took

out a bag full of gold and handed it to the old
man. "Take this," he said. "Your piece of brocade
is sold."

The old man hurried home with more thread
and all sorts of wonderful presents and good
things to eat.

"Look what I've brought home," he called happily, and he emptied all the gold coins still left in
the sack. "What a happy day for us," he said, and
he told the young girl how the lord had marveled
over her beautiful cloth.

The very next morning, the young girl again
went behind the screen and began to weave another piece of cloth. For three days the house was
filled with the sound of the loom, and again, on

the night of the third day, she finished another piece of brocade. The next morning, the old man went to the village and searched out the wealthy lord who lived at the top of the hill.

"I have another piece of brocade," the old man said, spreading out the second piece the girl had woven.

The lord looked at it carefully and exclaimed, "Why, this is even more beautiful than the last one." And without a moment's delay, he handed the old man an even bigger bag of gold.

The old man hurried home, laden with thread and gifts, and again they celebrated their good fortune with all kinds of good things to eat.

When the young girl went behind the screen for the third time to weave still another piece of brocade, the old woman could bear it no longer.

"I must take one little peek to see how she weaves that beautiful cloth," she said, and she got up to look behind the screen.

"But we promised," the old man warned. "We told her that we wouldn't look, no matter what happened."

But the old woman wouldn't listen. "Just one look won't hurt," she said, and she stole silently to the corner of the room and looked behind the screen.

She could hardly believe her eyes when she looked, for instead of the young girl she expected to see, she saw a great white stork standing before the loom. It was plucking its own soft white feathers and weaving them into the cloth with its long beak. The old woman saw that the bird had already plucked more than half of its feathers to make the beautiful white cloth.

"Ojii-san! Ojii-san!" she cried, running back to the old man, and she told him what she had seen behind the screen.

The old man shook his head sadly. "I told you not to look," he said. And the two old people sat silently, wondering about the strange sight the old woman had seen.

That night, the young girl came out from behind the screen carrying another beautiful piece of brocade. She sat before the old man and woman and bowed low.

"Thank you for being so good and kind to me," she said. "I am the stork the old man once saved in the snowstorm. Do you remember how you freed me from the trap?" she asked.

The old man nodded and the girl went on. "I wanted to repay you for saving my life, and so I decided to become a young girl and bring good fortune to your lives. But now I can no longer stay, for this morning Obaa-san saw me in my true form, and now you know my disguise."

The old woman hung her head. "Please forgive me," she murmured. "I was so anxious to see how you wove your cloth, I broke my promise to you and am very much ashamed."

"Please don't leave," the old man begged, but the young girl shook her head.

"I cannot stay," she said. "But I leave knowing that you will never be poor or hungry again. Good-bye, dear Ojii-san and Obaa-san."

Then she stepped outside and became once more a beautiful white bird. Glistening in the moonlight, she spread her wings out wide and flew high into the sky. Then, circling three times over the old man and woman, she soared off toward the stars and disappeared over the hills.

The old man and woman were lonely without the sweet young girl they had grown to love, but they remembered her always. And just as she had said, they were never poor or hungry again, and lived happily and comfortably ever after.

Acknowledgments

Grateful acknowledgment is made to the following authors and publishers for the use of copyrighted materials. Every effort has been made to obtain permission to use previously published material. Any errors or omissions are unintentional.

The Crossing Press for "The Boy Who Lived With the Bears" from *Iroquois Stories* as told by Joseph Bruchac. Text copyright © 1985 by Joseph Bruchac.

Harcourt Brace Jovanovich, Inc. for "Clever Manka" from *The Shepherd's Nosegay* by Parker Fillmore, copyright © 1958 and renewed 1986 by Harcourt Brace Jovanovich, Inc.

Harper & Row, Publishers, Inc. for "Zlateh the Goat" adapted from *Zlateh the Goat and Other Stories* by Isaac Bashevis Singer. Text copyright © 1966 by Isaac Bashevis Singer. Pictures copyright © 1966 by Maurice Sendak.

Yoshiko Uchida for "The Grateful Stork" from *The Magic Listening Cap and More Folk Tales From Japan* retold by Yoshiko Uchida. Copyright © 1955, 1983 Yoshiko Uchida.

Illustrations

Rae Ecklund: pp. 6-15; Maurice Sendak: pp. 16-29; Linda Graves: cover, pp. 30-39; Arvis Stewart: pp. 40-51; Christa Kieffer: pp. 52-63; Steve Cieslawski: pp. 64-79.